W9-BVR-607

10/2012

Dear Parent:
Your child's love of reading starts here!

Every child learns to read in a different way and at his or her own speed. Some go back and forth between reading levels and read favorite books again and again. Others read through each level in order. You can help your young reader improve and become more confident by encouraging his or her own interests and abilities. From books your child reads with you to the first books he or she reads alone, there are I Can Read Books for every stage of reading:

SHARED READING
Basic language, word repetition, and whimsical illustrations, ideal for sharing with your emergent reader

BEGINNING READING
Short sentences, familiar words, and simple concepts for children eager to read on their own

READING WITH HELP
Engaging stories, longer sentences, and language play for developing readers

READING ALONE
Complex plots, challenging vocabulary, and high-interest topics for the independent reader

ADVANCED READING
Short paragraphs, chapters, and exciting themes for the perfect bridge to chapter books

I Can Read Books have introduced children to the joy of reading since 1957. Featuring award-winning authors and illustrators and a fabulous cast of beloved characters, I Can Read Books set the standard for beginning readers.

A lifetime of discovery begins with the magical words **"I Can Read!"**

Visit www.icanread.com for information
on enriching your child's reading experience.

For Callum—

Do you ever stand still?

—R.S.

I Can Read Book® is a trademark of HarperCollins Publishers.

Splat the Cat: The Rain Is a Pain
Copyright © 2012 by Rob Scotton
All rights reserved. Manufactured in China.

Library of Congress catalog card number: 2012937968
ISBN 978-0-06-209018-8 (trade bdg.) —ISBN 978-0-06-209017-1 (pbk.)

12 13 14 15 16   SCP   10 9 8 7 6 5 4 3 2 1

First Edition

Splat the Cat
The Rain Is a Pain

Based on the bestselling books
by Rob Scotton

Cover art by Rob Scotton

Text by Amy Hsu Lin

Interior illustrations by Robert Eberz

HARPER
An Imprint of HarperCollinsPublishers

Splat couldn't wait

to spend a whole day

in his brand-new skates.

It was a sunny day.

There was one plain little cloud

in the sky,

but it looked far away.

Splat jumped, spun, and flipped,
and the cloud got bigger.

It got closer. It got darker.

Splat tried to skate away.

He went left.

He went right.

But the cloud followed.

It was gaining on him.

Now the cloud looked

as big as a plane

or a train.

It was gray.

It was a dark, stormy gray.

The cloud poured rain.

"The rain is a pain!"

Splat complained.

Inside, Splat tried to dry off.

He shook out his fur.

He jiggled his paws.

He squeezed his tail.

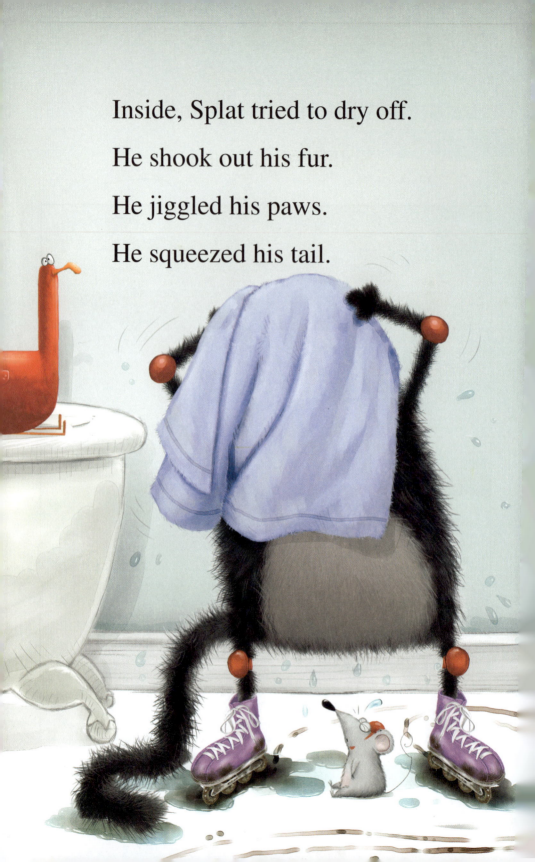

But Splat was still very wet.

"I'll just air-dry," he said,

standing in a big muddy puddle.

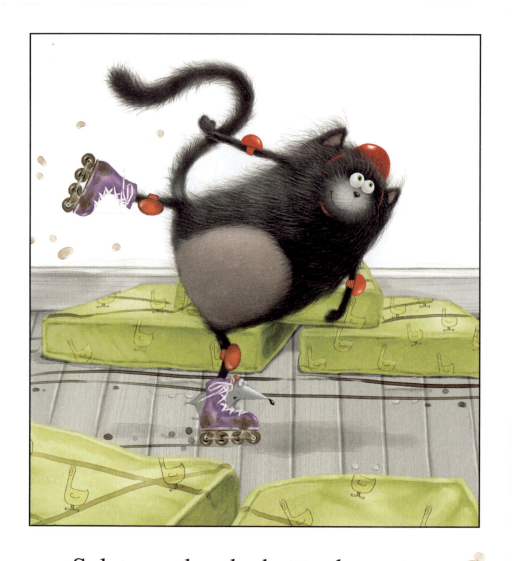

Splat wondered what to do next.

"Use your brain," he told himself.

He rolled into the living room

and built a racetrack.

14

Splat went faster and faster,

around and around and around.

SPLAT!

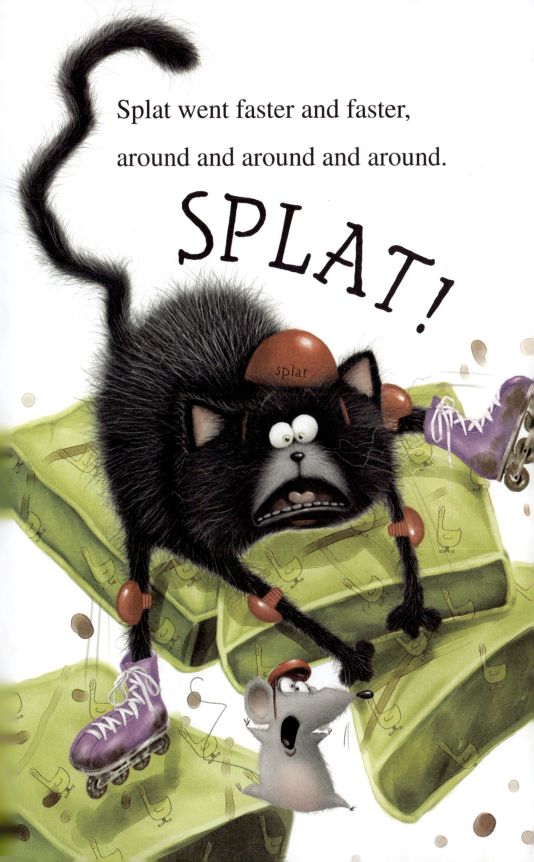

Splat picked up one muddy paw,

and then another.

He left a big muddy puddle

and a big muddy stain.

Mom was not happy.

"Out, Splat, out!" she said.

"But it's pouring," Splat explained.

"The rain is a pain!"

All the skating had made Splat hungry.

He rolled to the kitchen

for some ice cream.

Little Sis was frosting fish sticks.

Little Sis had the radio on.

"Meow Rock" began to play.

It was Splat's favorite song!

He began to sing and dance.

Splat bumped into Little Sis.

The frosting spilled everywhere.

"Out, Splat, out!" said Little Sis.

"I can't go out," said Splat.

"The rain is a pain!"

Splat rolled into the dining room.

The song made him think

of something to do.

"Let's play musical chairs,"

Splat said to Seymour.

Splat fell flat.

Dad was not happy.

"Out, Splat, out!" he said.

"It's still pouring," said Splat.

"The rain is a pain!"

Splat rolled into the hall

to take off his skates.

But Splat ran into Little Sis.

SPLAT!

Her plate of frosted fish sticks

went flying!

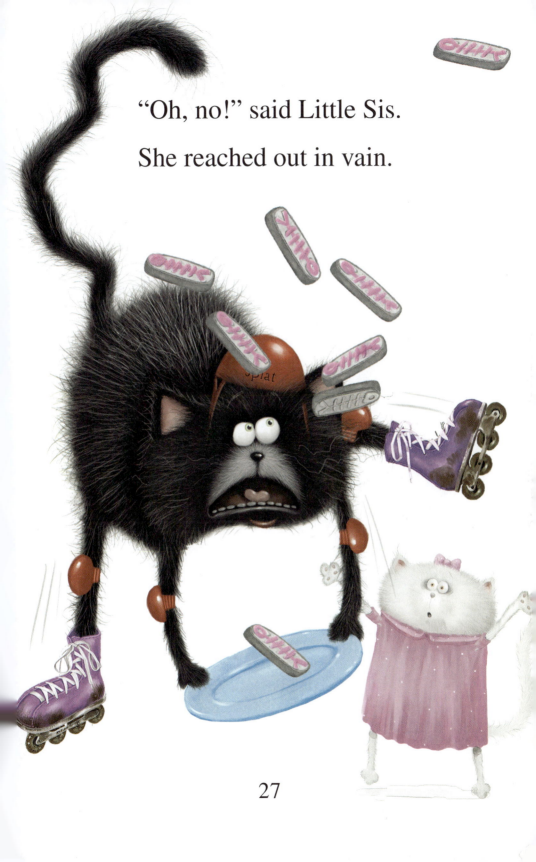

"Oh, no!" said Little Sis.

She reached out in vain.

27

"Yikes!" yelled Splat.

But he caught the plate!

All the fish sticks remained.

Mom and Dad heard the shouting.

They rushed in and ran into Splat.

Fish sticks went everywhere.

Everyone slipped on the fish sticks.

Everyone slid in the muddy puddles,

down the hall and out the door.

"Oh, no!" said Splat. "The rain . . .

. . . makes a rainbow!"